the Sea of Bath

by Bob Logan

sourcebooks
jabberwocky

Published by Sourcebooks Jabberwocky, an imprint of Sourcebooks, Inc.
P.O. Box 4410, Naperville, Illinois 60567-4410
(630) 961-3900
Fax: (630) 961-2168
www.jabberwockykids.com

Library of Congress Cataloging-in-Publication data is on file with the publisher.

Source of Production: Oceanic Graphic Printing, Kowloon, Hong Kong
Date of Production: September 2010
Run Number: 12894

Printed and bound in China.
OGP 10 9 8 7 6 5 4 3 2 1

To my son, Jack

The Captain was asleep on his boat...

...when the tide came in.

He has sailed this sea many times before.

It is a curious sea, indeed!

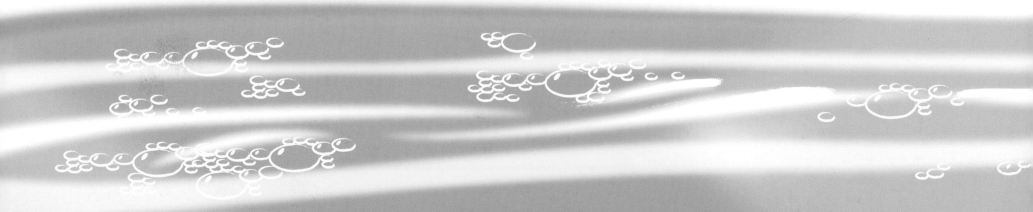

It is a sea where ducks SQUEAK instead of QUACK...

...and deep-sea divers chase crocodiles...

...while bubble-blowing bears chase deep-sea divers!

The Captain often wonders about this strange sea and its travelers.

Do drops from the sky mean rain?

Or does a cheerful whale want to play fetch?

Do bouncy waves mean a storm is brewing?

Or are ships engaged in a friendly sea battle?

S.S. Rubb A. Dubb

Does this odd little boat by
the name of *Soap* wish to race?

A push from this sea creature
helps the Captain take the lead!

SOAP

When the Captain's voyage comes to an end—it always ends the same...

The sea gets *lower*...

And lower...

And lower...

Until the sea is gone.

Will the Captain ever learn what sea he sails?

Perhaps tomorrow.